The Cave of the Lost Fraggle

By Michael Teitelbaum • Pictures by Peter Elwell

Muppet Press
Holt, Rinehart and Winston
NEW YORK

Published by Holt, Rinehart and Winston,
383 Madison Avenue, New York, New York 10017.

Library of Congress Cataloging in Publication Data
Teitelbaum, Michael.
The cave of the lost fraggle.
Summary: Red Fraggle accepts a dare to explore the
Cave of the Lost Fraggle, from which no fraggle has
ever returned.
1. Children's stories, American.   [1. Puppets—
Fiction.   2. Caves—Fiction.]   I. Elwell, Peter, ill.
II. Title.
PZ7.T233Cav   1985   [E]   84-18939
ISBN: 0-03-004554-1

First Edition
Printed in the United States of America
1 3 5 7 9 10 8 6 4 2

ISBN 0-03-004554-1

The Cave of the Lost Fraggle

"LAST one in is a . . . a . . . A GORG!" shouted Red Fraggle, as she raced along a path and leaped into the Fraggle Pond. Last One In was one of Red's favorite games.

"My turn," said Gobo. "Last one in is . . . A STALE DOOZER STICK!" he shouted, as he hit the water with a splash. "Hey, Red. I think that one was even better than yours!"

"It was not!" said Red.

"It was, too!" said Gobo.

"Oh, yeah?" said Red. "Let's try it again."

"Fine with me," said Gobo. "Ready, set, go!" The two Fraggles ran down the path and jumped high into the air.

"Last one in is a SLIMY POND WORM!" screamed Red.

"Last one in is a SILLY CREATURE!" Gobo said at the same time.

"Ker-splash!" they both went as they landed in the Pond.

"There," said Gobo. "That settles it. I'm better at this game than you are."

"I think Gobo's got you there, Red," said Wembley, who had been watching.

"What!" exclaimed Red.

"Well, maybe not," began Wembley. "I mean . . ."

Red turned back to Gobo.

"Gobo Fraggle," she said, "you are not better than me . . . at anything!"

"Oh, yeah?" said Gobo, who was beginning to get a little angry himself. "What about exploring? You've never even been to Outer Space! And—"

Red cut him off. "Well, you're not such a hotshot explorer, Gobo. *You've* never even explored the Cave of the Lost Fraggle!"

The Fraggles all gasped. No one had ever returned from exploring the Cave of the Lost Fraggle. Legend had it that the strange echoes in the Cave were the voices of Fraggles who had lost their way trying to get out.

"Come on, Red," said Gobo. "You know that not even Uncle Matt would try to explore *that* terrible place."

"Well, I bet you I could do it!" Red boasted.

"All right, Red Fraggle," Gobo said. "You asked for it. I *dare* you to explore the Cave of the Lost Fraggle!"

Everyone gasped again. A Fraggle dare was never taken lightly.

"I accept!" said Red, as she stormed away.

Later that day, Red was in her room packing. All her friends were there, too.

"Oh, Red," Mokey cried. "Please don't go!"

"We'll never see you again!" moaned Boober.

"Red," said Gobo, "I wasn't really serious. This is silly."

"You should have thought about that before you dared me. No Fraggle has ever gone back on a dare! And Red Fraggle is not going to be the first!" With that, Red took her pack and left the cave.

Gobo looked at his friends helplessly. "I should never have dared Red," he said, shaking his head. "I hope she'll be okay."

Although Red's journey took only half a day,
it was not an easy one. She crossed the River of
the Raging Rapids . . .

. . . the Mountain of Many Mysteries . . .

. . . and the Marsh of the Mushy Mushrooms.

Finally, she arrived at the entrance to the Cave of the Lost Fraggle. She looked into the opening. *It doesn't look so scary,* she thought. *It's just another cave. This will be easy.*

Red made her way along the twisting maze. She turned left and then right.

She followed paths that led deep into the earth and then climbed back up again. Hours passed.

This isn't so terrible, she thought. *I am Red the Great, Explorer of Caves—the first Fraggle ever to return from the Cave of the Lost Fraggle!*

After she had walked a long while, Red stopped in one of
the many rooms and opened her pack. The radishes that
Mokey had given her for lunch tasted delicious. As she
chewed, she looked around. *This place is boring,* she thought.
Every room looks the same.

"I think I've explored enough!" she decided after she had
finished eating. "I guess I'll go home now." She stood up and
looked around. That was when she realized something. She
couldn't remember which way she had come. Every room *did*
look the same!

Red's tail started to sweat, and her heart began to pound.
I have to go left. I'm sure I recognize that rock, she thought.

Or is it right? That rock looks exactly the same! Oh, why did I accept that stupid dare in the first place?

Red was hopelessly lost.

Suddenly, Red heard a noise. "Aoooo!" it went. "What's that?" Red said out loud. Maybe it was a Voice of a Lost Fraggle! Red shivered. Would she become a Lost Fraggle, too—destined to wander the Cave forever?

Red heard another noise. This time, it was definitely a voice. *"Halloo!"* it said.

"It *is* the Voices of the Lost Fraggles!" cried Red, now completely terrified. "I'm doomed!"

Red grabbed her pack and was about to run when the voice
called again. *"Red!"* it shouted.

Oh, no! Red thought. *They already know my name!*

Red stopped short. *Wait a minute!* she thought. *How can they know my name?*

And then she recognized the voice.

"Gobo!" she cried out loud. "It's Gobo! Gobo! I'm here!"
"Stay where you are and keep talking. We'll get you out!"
Gobo's voice was faint but clear.

"Oh, Gobo," Red said sadly. "It was really dumb of me to run
off like that. I don't even know how it happened. And I never
want to explore another cave again. I just want to go home!"
At that moment, Gobo appeared.

And Gobo wasn't alone. Behind him were Wembley, Mokey, and Boober!

"Boy, am I glad to see you!" Red cried, hugging her good friends. "How did you get here so fast?"

"Actually, we left right after you did," Gobo said sheepishly. "We were really worried about you. Red, I never should have dared you in the first place.

"Dares aren't just dumb . . . they can make you do things that are dangerous. So let's get out of here, okay?"

"But how are we going to get out again?" Red asked.

"Come on," said Gobo. "I'll show you."

Gobo took Red by the hand. Then he linked hands with Wembley. Wembley took Mokey's hand, and Mokey took Boober's. Boober was already holding Large Marvin's hand. Gobo had formed a chain of Fraggles that led to the entrance of the Cave!

"Ready!" he cried. Slowly, the chain began to move. And in a little while, all the Fraggles were outside the Cave again.

"Are we all here?" Gobo asked.

Everybody was.

After all the Fraggles had congratulated Gobo and hugged Red, Gobo spoke up again.

"Okay," he said. "Everybody back to the Pond. And the last one in is a . . . a . . . a Lost Fraggle!"

The Fraggles all laughed—especially Red. Then they all raced back to the Fraggle Pond!

The End